EMOJI OF DOOM

EVAN JACOBS

SADDLEBACK
EDUCATIONAL PUBLISHING

WH/TE L/GHTNING
BOOKS

SADDLEBACK
EDUCATIONAL PUBLISHING
www.sdlback.com

ISBN-13: 978-1-68021-354-6
ISBN-10: 1-68021-354-7
eBook: 978-1-63078-778-3

Printed in Malaysia

21 20 19 18 17   1 2 3 4 5

EMOJI FACTS

WORLD
EMOJI DAY!

JULY
17

絵文字えもじ

THE WORD **EMOJI** IS TAKEN FROM JAPANESE.
"E" MEANS **PICTURE**
"MOJI" MEANS **CHARACTER**

;) A SMILEY FACE EMOJI DATES ALL THE WAY BACK TO 1862!

DICTIONARY

"EMOJI" WAS OFFICIALLY
ADDED AS A WORD TO
DICTIONARIES IN 2013.

EMOJIS PEOPLE USE INCORRECTLY

"Dead"
ACTUAL MEANING: SHOCKED

"FIRE"
ACTUAL MEANING: NAME BADGE

CHAPTER 1

Dyre High School. It was lunchtime. Travis Parker was sitting with his girlfriend, Sonya Vasquez. Next to Sonya was her best friend, Carla O'Neill. Travis's best friend, Erik Pitram, was there too.

"You can talk about anything except Walk the Moon!" Travis laughed. He hated that band.

"*Shut up and dance with me!*" Erik sang with a grin. He stood up. Then he waved his hands in the air.

"Please stop!" Travis pleaded.

"This woman is my destiny ..." Sonya crooned. She finished the line Erik had started. She wrapped her arms around Carla as she sang.

Walk the Moon's big hit was "Shut Up and Dance." If Travis heard it again, he would scream.

Erik ran a hand through his thick black hair. He kept it shaved down on the sides. It looked like he had a mohawk. The boy certainly liked to keep himself in style. This year he was all about wearing light blue denim. He sat back down at the table.

Travis pulled up his hoodie. It said "Dyre Varsity Basketball" across the chest. He'd been on the varsity team since sophomore year. He was one of the team's best players.

"Are you hiding?" Carla laughed.

Carla and Sonya liked to dress alike. They wore yoga pants and T-shirts. Sonya let her dark brown hair hang down her back. Carla always pulled her long black hair into a ponytail.

Sonya, Erik, and Carla were all in theater.

That fall they were in the play *The Legend of Sleepy Hollow*.

"Yeah, I'm hiding." Travis pulled on the strings of his hoodie. The hood tightened against his head. He pretended to scan the other tables, looking for his fans. "You guys are going to ruin my rep."

"You're such a dork," Sonya said. She threw a piece of bread at him.

It bounced off his shoulder. Travis picked it up and ate it.

He was always hungry. The chicken sandwich and fries were not enough. Sonya and Carla ate pizza. Erik never ate lunch at school. He never seemed to eat. Ever.

"Like you have a rep to ruin," Carla said.

"We're classing you up, fool!" Erik said.

"Not if you're singing that song," Travis said.

"Don't make me sing it again." Erik moved like he was going to stand up.

"No! Please!" Travis put his hands together. It looked like he was praying.

They all laughed. The foursome always had a good time together. Erik and Carla flirted. A lot. But they were only good friends.

Travis took out his phone. He started scrolling through his emails. He had been thinking about colleges. There were so many questions. Could he get a scholarship? That was the main question. His family wasn't rich. They weren't poor either.

UCLA was his number one. Travis knew it was expensive. USC was another pick, and even pricier.

Travis had sent each admissions office a letter. In it he wrote about why he wanted to go to college. He'd included some YouTube links of his basketball games. The clips showed him scoring. Travis was known to hustle. The videos showed that too.

Had any of the colleges responded to his emails?

"You checking for that emoji?" Erik laughed.

"Stop!" Carla said. She reached over to Erik. Then she covered his mouth with her hand. He moved it away.

"Girl, your skin feels good."

Carla rolled her eyes.

"What emoji?" Travis asked. He didn't look up from his phone.

"You guys don't know about this?" Erik looked at them. "The emoji email is a chain letter. Like the old paper letters. You know, the ones your parents used to get."

"Letters?" Carla said. "Who sends letters? That's so eighties!"

"You won't be saying that if you get one," Erik went on. "This thing is bad. Like really bad. If you get one, you have to send it to three people in twenty-four hours. If you don't, you'll be cursed. You will have bad luck."

Travis looked up. "For how long?" he asked.

"I don't know. How long do curses last?" Erik

had their attention now. "Also, supposedly you can't see who sent you the emoji. It's set up that way."

"You're such a liar," Travis said. He looked back down at his phone.

"Okay, but if you get one—"

"You'll be the first person I send it to," Travis said.

"Remember when you told us the school was haunted? This is totally bogus, Erik," Sonya said.

"Or that other time?" Carla said. "Our new English teacher didn't come back after winter break. You told everyone she'd died."

"I thought she did," Erik said matter-of-factly. "And have either of you ever been here late at night? I have. It's scary!"

The bell sounded. Lunch was over.

Erik and Carla walked off into the mass of students.

Sonya walked up to Travis. "Call me after practice," she said.

"Always," Travis said.

They kissed. Travis and Sonya smiled at each other. Then they went their separate ways.

CHAPTER 2

*T*hump. *Thump. Thump.*

The sound of basketballs echoed across the gym. Coach Hua split the team in two. Half practiced defense. The other half did layup drills.

The players loved Coach Hua. He was young. And he didn't dress like the other coaches. Coach usually wore T-shirts and chinos. Vans were his shoes of choice. The coach had graduated from Dyre. During his senior year, Coach had won a basketball state championship.

It was almost an hour into practice. The guys were sweaty. Travis's jersey clung to his body. During the layup drills, he barely missed one. He had inspired the other guys to do better too.

On the shooting drills, nobody could stop him. Travis always managed to get around a blocker. He was easily the best player on an A+ team. So far they were 11–1 for the season.

Practice ended around 5:00 p.m.

The players hit the showers. All of them except Travis. He stayed behind and ran up and down the court. He also practiced his free throws. His eyes were on the prize: going to a good college.

Basketball was his golden ticket.

"You get it yet?" Tony Slocum asked as he played with his phone.

Travis and Tony were lab partners in AP Chemistry. Paired students worked at tables.

The teacher, Mr. Nguyen, sat at his desk. He was grading papers. Every so often he'd look up at the students. The kids were focused. The teacher didn't have to worry about his AP students goofing off.

Travis worked through an equation. He and Tony took turns. "Almost," Travis said.

Tony cracked up.

"What?" Travis asked.

"Nothing," Tony said. He continued laughing.

"You're laughing at nothing?" Travis went back to the equation. Normally he could figure it out. Now he couldn't for some reason.

"Look at this," Tony said. He held up his phone. An emoji was on the screen. The emoji was smiling. It was black with red teeth. Blank white eyes with no pupils stared at them.

"Huh? I guess that's funny," Travis said.

"You haven't heard about this?" Tony asked.

"I have. It's supposed to be bad if you don't send it out."

"You believe it?" Tony asked.

"No," Travis said. "I mean, look at that thing."

Tony held up his phone again. They both stared at the emoji. "It's stupid," Tony said. Then he deleted it from his phone.

CHAPTER 3

Travis, Sonya, Erik, and Carla were at the football game. Dyre was playing Motley High. It was an away game, but many Dyre students showed up.

Dyre was getting trounced. The team had a winning record, but that's not how they were playing. Motley was ahead 21–0. It was only the first half.

The night was super cold. Fans from both schools had bundled up. Nobody felt like cheering. "Whenever you guys want to leave ..." Erik said.

"You're such a jerk." Carla hit him playfully. "Show some spirit."

"If the basketball team were getting killed, would you bail?" Travis eyed Erik.

"No," Erik said. "But you're my boy. I don't know any of those players."

Suddenly everybody in the stands gasped.

"What happened?" Travis scanned the field.

"I think someone got hurt," Sonya said.

Everyone stood up.

There was a crowd of players on the field. Some Dyre players pushed some Motley players. The fans started yelling. The coaches joined the referee on the field. The pushing stopped. Players moved away from each other.

Travis could see a first aid team. There was a crowd around the injured Dyre player.

"Who is it?" Travis asked.

"It's hard to see," Erik said.

"It's Number 13," someone said.

Number 13? That was Tony.

Erik's mom had come to drive them home. She sat alone up front. The four teens were in the back of the minivan.

"Well," Erik said. "That was brutal."

"Yeah, I hope Tony's okay," Sonya said.

"Me too," Travis agreed.

"You're just bummed being out a lab partner," Erik said.

"You're an idiot," Travis said.

"You're the fool that took AP Chem."

"Forgive me for wanting to go to a good school when I graduate."

"It was weird seeing Tony injured like that," Carla said.

"I know," Sonya said. "On a stretcher! It didn't look like he was moving."

"He'll be okay," Erik said. "He's a football player. They're tough."

There was silence after Erik said that.

Ding. Ding.

"Apparently he's not as tough as you thought," Sonya said. "Kimmy just texted me. Tony almost broke his back. He's going to be out the rest of the season."

"That's a lie!" Erik shot back.

Kimmy Molina was Tony's girlfriend. She and Sonya had been best friends when they were younger. They were still friendly now. Kimmy didn't have any reason to lie. Tony had been badly injured.

CHAPTER 4

After basketball practice Travis walked home. He was deep in thought. All the students in Mr. Nguyen's AP Chemistry class were already paired off. This meant that Travis would be without a lab partner.

He didn't mind. Travis just felt bad that Tony had gotten hurt. Tony was a talented player. The team would have a hard time without him.

His thoughts turned to Sonya. They had been dating for almost six months. He wanted to do something special for their anniversary. It was in three weeks.

His parents paid him for doing household chores. Travis had been saving his money for a while. He almost had three hundred dollars. Travis wanted to take Sonya to a fancy steakhouse. He just needed another hundred dollars. The restaurant was expensive. Sonya would be so impressed!

Travis knew he could make more money if he had a part-time job. He planned to get one his senior year. Life would be easier then. SATs would be done. So would his college applications. He wouldn't feel so much pressure. Maybe he'd get an acceptance letter before senior year even began.

Buzz. Buzz.

Travis looked at his phone. It was an email. He opened it without thinking. What if it was a college scout?

The subject line was blank. There was no sender. Huh?

There it was. In the middle of the email message. The emoji! The same one Tony had received. It had the same red teeth. Its eyes were white and lifeless.

Tony thought the message was a joke. He had deleted it. Now he was out for the season. Was it because of the emoji? Travis couldn't help but wonder.

Empty white eyes stared at Travis. Was the emoji alive? What was it waiting for?

Travis couldn't delete it. But he didn't want to send it to anyone either. The twenty-four hour clock was ticking. He had to do something.

Four days later Travis deleted the emoji email. He didn't tell anyone. It didn't mean anything. The emoji was a sick joke. No way would he pass it on. So far nothing bad had happened.

After that day's basketball practice, Travis told Sonya. He was walking home when he called her.

"You did?" she asked.

Sonya always did her homework after school. Travis could hear her music in the background.

"Why take so long to tell me?" she asked.

"I don't know," he said. "I guess I was shaken up about Tony."

"You don't really think an emoji has any power, do you?" She laughed. "Erik was totally lying. You called him out that day at lunch."

"I guess I felt bad for Tony," Travis said sheepishly. "I play a sport. What if I got hurt like he did? It would totally blow for me."

"You're so dramatic, Travis. You should be in drama, not on the basketball team."

"Well, I deleted it today."

"I can't believe you think that's why Tony got hurt," Sonya said.

"I don't," he said. "I was just being cautious."

"Uh-huh. Well, don't be too cautious," Sonya

said. "Are you still planning our anniversary dinner? You told me it would be epic."

"It will be. Just get ready," he said. "Be prepared for a night you will never forget."

"I can't wait."

CHAPTER 5

Travis knew something was odd the minute he got home. He didn't see his dad's car in the driveway. He went inside.

His parents sat at the kitchen table. The kitchen was next to the living room. A hallway from the living room connected all the bedrooms.

Travis's dad was still in his suit. He'd unbuttoned his shirt. There was an icepack on his neck. Papers covered the kitchen table. His briefcase was on the floor next to his chair.

His mom wore her yoga gear. She liked to practice every afternoon when she got home from work.

"Hey," Travis said cautiously. "Is everything okay?"

"I had a car accident," his dad said. "A bad one."

"Are you hurt?" Travis sat down.

"Just a little," his dad said. "But the car is totaled."

"You should've seen it, Travis," his mom said. "I'm glad your father's okay. I'm also relieved it's not his fault."

"This truck just came out of nowhere," his dad said.

"I'm glad you're okay," Travis said.

"Thanks. I know you wanted to borrow the nicer car."

"Yeah," Travis said, sighing.

Travis had counted the days for his provisional driver's license to expire. He was *so* ready to drive with his friends. His father's car was new. Well, not anymore. It was a heap of metal.

Travis couldn't drive Sonya to the steakhouse in his mom's old car. He wasn't a snob. But it would be embarrassing. Without his dad's car, the anniversary date wouldn't be nearly as special.

Was the emoji to blame? Maybe he shouldn't have deleted it.

"You *still* haven't sent it out!" Erik yelled.

Erik walked with Travis. The two were going to their first class. Other students stared at them since Erik was so emotional.

"Shh." Travis held his finger up to his lips. "I can't. It's been over a week."

"If you still had time, would you?" Erik asked.

"I don't know. Probably not."

"Travis …" Erik's expression turned serious. "I'm telling you, bro. Do not mess with this emoji."

"Bro?" Travis laughed. He couldn't believe how dramatic Erik was being.

"This is serious." Erik's tone changed. "I'm superstitious. You don't want to mess with this stuff."

"I'm not. I'm not doing anything." Travis couldn't believe it. Erik was dead serious.

"I know," Erik said. "That's the problem."

Travis went to bed two hours later than normal. After finishing his homework, he looked at college applications. No word yet about his YouTube clips.

Panic gripped him as he looked over the information. The financial aid application was intense. He was so confused. The language was puzzling.

He finally gave up. There was no point in worrying. But he couldn't turn off his brain. Sleep did not come. Would any of his choice schools accept him?

Maybe the bad luck would continue. It was because of that emoji …

"Don't be stupid," he said out loud.

Eventually Travis dozed off.

Travis was in the high school gym. He was playing basketball. Who was he playing? He couldn't tell. The other team wore dark red uniforms. The score was 330–332.

What?! It made no sense. No team ever scored this many points, let alone two teams in an almost tie.

A teammate passed the ball to Travis. Travis made his way to the basket. The players in red tried to defend it.

Somehow Travis moved past them.

Then he leaped into the air.

Swish!

He dunked the ball. Travis knew this had to be a dream. He never dunked the ball.

He turned and smiled at his teammates. But something was wrong. Every player had morphed. Their skin was green. Blood ran from some of their mouths. Others oozed blood from their ears. Chunks of skin plopped onto the court. Limbs seemed disconnected from bodies. Rivers of blood flowed to the exits.

The creepy players moved toward Travis. Their movements were slow.

Someone tossed Travis the basketball. He instinctively caught it. Only it wasn't a basketball. It was the emoji!

It opened and closed its mouth. The emoji's red teeth chomped. Then it ate Travis's hand!

Its teeth were razors. The emoji easily cut through Travis's bones. Its white eyes remained lifeless.

"Aahh!" Travis screamed. He'd never felt pain like this. But weirdly, there was no blood. At least not from him. The emoji moved up his arm. Every bite was intensely painful.

Travis knew it was a dream. But he couldn't wake up!

The emoji chomped away. When it got to

Travis's shoulder, its jaws seemed to unhinge. Its red teeth were closing in on Travis's head.

"No!" Travis cried.

And then he woke up.

CHAPTER 6

Y ou dreamed that an emoji was eating you?" Sonya laughed. "You've been hanging out with Erik too much, Travis."

The two were going to lunch. Sonya was driving. He hadn't told her about his dad's car accident. Travis knew she would offer her car for their big date. He wanted them to go to dinner in style. There were two weeks left to figure it out.

"Yeah," he said. "It was crazy! I could actually feel it eating me."

Sonya burst out laughing. Travis looked at her.

"Sorry, babe." She put her hand on his shoulder. "It just sounds so weird."

"You're telling me," he said. "I woke up drenched in sweat. The dream felt so real. As it was eating its way up my arm, I wanted to wake up. But I couldn't."

"So how'd you finally wake up?" Sonya asked.

"I don't know."

Sonya drove to Taco Bell. Travis wasn't hungry. She did her best to cheer him up. Sonya could make Travis laugh. She told him about a show she was watching. She acted out some of the scenes. Sonya was great at improv. Before he knew it they were back on campus. Travis had forgotten all about the evil emoji.

Until he got another email.

"Dude," Erik said. The boys were in Erik's bedroom. "This one is way worse."

Erik lived in a big house with his parents,

grandma, and three brothers. It was chaos. His room was a mess. Piles of clothes. Pictures of his many friends. Stacks of books. Erik also had a large flat-screen TV and a few tablets.

They sat across from Erik's desktop computer. Travis stared at the new emoji. It was almost identical to the first. It was black. Its teeth were red. It had one open eye. The other eye was just a line.

"Shut up," Travis said. "I'm seriously freaked out here."

Travis was glad Coach Hua had moved practice back an hour. He couldn't practice with this new emoji on his mind. Erik had asked him to come over. Travis hoped they could figure something out.

"I know." Erik didn't smile. "So am I." He pointed to the computer screen. The browser showed a wiki page about emojis and their meanings. "When did you get this?" Erik asked.

"After lunch."

"At one thirty?"

"Yeah," Travis said.

"Well, it's a little after three." Erik looked at Travis. He seemed genuinely worried. "You still have time."

"Time?" Travis was confused.

"To send it out," Erik said. "Travis! You only have six hours with the second one. If you don't, your bad luck will get worse."

"It's not that bad—"

"Your dad was in a car accident! How can that not be bad?"

"So if I send it out, everything will be okay?" The boys stared at each other. "Dude, that sounds crazy."

"It won't be okay. You didn't send out the first one. As punishment it says you'll be cursed with a year of bad luck. You only get one more chance. If you don't send out this second emoji …" Erik started clicking around his computer.

"What?" Travis snapped. He was starting to

get nervous. It was like the same fear he'd felt in his dream. "What happens?"

"Whoa! Check this out," Erik said.

YouTube launched. There were hundreds of videos. Each one related to the emojis. Travis scanned the titles.

Life Is Hell

Ignore at Your Own Risk

Get It, Send It!

"How many videos are there?" Travis asked.

"A lot."

Erik clicked on one. A girl appeared on the screen. She had ignored the first emoji. How stupid, she said. Then another came. She ignored it too.

Then her little sister drowned.

Erik clicked the next video. A boy appeared. He had ignored all the emojis. Then he started crying. His dad had lost his job. His mom had lost hers too. The family was now homeless. They moved into a hotel. But that was too expensive. His parents argued. Now they were divorcing.

All because he had ignored the emoji emails.

Erik clicked on a few more. The stories were the same. Ignore the emojis and bad things would happen. Live in a nightmare.

A girl spoke about being attacked by the emoji. It had come after her. When anyone was around, it disappeared. It had even tried to eat her.

"It kept coming," she said. "It won't ever stop."

Travis left Erik's house. He had to go to basketball practice. Travis was torn. The emoji was silly. But at the same time, he had a lot of plans. He wanted to get good grades. Go to a good school. He wanted great things to happen for him and Sonya. Was he dissing all those goals?

But he couldn't send out the emoji. Travis didn't want to give anyone bad luck. Fear was for wimps. The Internet was full of phonies. Maybe everything he saw with Erik was faked. It was impossible to know.

The clock ticked. Six hours flew by.

And Travis still hadn't sent out one emoji.

CHAPTER 7

We *look forward to seeing you play in tomorrow night's game against Hillside."*

Travis couldn't believe what he was reading. He had checked his email between classes. UCLA had emailed him back! It was his first choice.

The school would send a scout to the game. The email was vague. It didn't say if Travis would meet the scout. He didn't care. This was his shot. His dream had potential. He could not blow it.

If he played the best game of his career, the

scout would see it. A scholarship was within his reach!

"So much for bad luck," he said.

Travis made his way to calculus. He had ignored the emoji emails. Blocked them from his mind. The bad luck had been a coincidence. There was no such thing as a curse. He felt like he had done the right thing.

Travis was terrible in practice. Why?

Bronson Haydel.

Bronson was new to Dyer. At his old school, he was a star player. Bronson was tall. Travis was six foot two. The other boy was easily four inches taller.

Coach usually told his players about incoming players. But not this time. Bronson was a surprise. And like Travis, Bronson played center. Everything Travis did, Bronson did three hundred times better.

Coach organized a scrimmage. Travis made a

free throw. Bronson made a three-pointer. Travis made a layup. Bronson dunked the ball. Travis had hustle. Bronson was better in every way.

"He's got mad hops," one player said.

Travis was done. Bronson continued to practice.

"Yeah," Travis said. He took a sip of water. Normally he would be the guy still on the court. But he didn't feel like it today.

He did his best to be happy. Travis was a team player. Ultimately he just wanted to win. He thought about the scout coming to watch him play. Travis was just as good as Bronson. Wasn't he? Or had he used up all his luck? Maybe ...

It was the next night. He barely played against Hillside. Bronson seemed to score every other point. Had Coach forgotten about him?

The gym was packed with people. All eyes were on Bronson. He was the star player now.

Travis's parents were there. They smiled

when he looked at them. He knew what they were thinking. Their son should be playing more.

The clock counted down. Travis could barely stomach watching it. He wondered where the scout sat. What would he say if could meet the scout? He couldn't tell him about his bad luck. An evil emoji had put a better player on the team.

"Parker, you're in!" Coach said. There were three minutes left. Dyre was up by 15 points.

Travis could barely think. His big chance with UCLA was drifting away. His teammates weren't passing the ball to him. And when they did, Travis missed each shot!

Hillcrest started to rally. But it was too late. Bronson had made it impossible for them to win.

The buzzer sounded. The game was over.

Travis had bombed in front of everyone. But Dyre had still won. And it was all because of Bronson.

"It wasn't so bad," Sonya said. She hugged Travis as they walked toward his parents.

The gym was almost empty. Bronson had already left. Travis had seen him talking with an unfamiliar man. Was he the UCLA scout? Had Bronson taken his spot?

"Yes, it was that bad," he said. "I didn't even play. And when I did—"

"Did you talk to the scout?" his mom asked.

"You did well," his dad lied. "You didn't have enough time to get going."

Travis could tell his dad was unhappy. He was disappointed in his son.

"I'm going to shower," Travis said. He looked at Sonya. "I'll meet you in ten minutes."

The showers steamed up the locker room. Travis dressed slowly. He put on a white T-shirt and shorts. He threw on his Dyre hoodie. Then he shut his locker.

Travis walked out of the locker room. Huh?

The gym was still open. He could see a sliver of light through the doors. People were laughing.

He went into the gym. But it was empty. The bleachers were stowed. He looked around. Then he heard a dripping sound. What was it? He looked around. It wasn't raining. Where was it coming from? Was there a leak somewhere?

Travis walked to the center of the court. The dripping sound was louder. He looked up. No way! He blinked.

It wasn't a leak.

There was blood. It dripped from one of the basketball nets. Blood pooled under the net.

Travis walked over to it. "What the heck " he said.

Suddenly he heard a buzzing sound. The gym's lights had been switched on. They were getting bright. The buzzing got louder.

He started sweating. The lights burned hot.

Thump. Thump. Thump.

It was like a thousand basketballs being

dribbled at once. Travis turned around. There were no basketballs.

It was the emoji. Just like in his dream! The emoji was huge. And it was getting bigger!

Thump. Thump. Thump.

It pounded against the court.

The emoji's white eyes got wider. It smiled, revealing dark red teeth.

Thump. Crack. Thump. Crack.

The gym's floor split in half. The crack widened. Travis turned and ran. He was so close to the exit. As he ran, the floor continued to collapse.

The emoji bounced after him.

The floor opened up before he could escape. Travis looked into nothingness. There was no bottom to the deep crack.

"Aahh!" he screamed as he fell into the abyss.

Then there was nothing. No dripping. No lights. No thumping.

Travis sat up. He looked around. The gym was back to normal. He got up quickly.

"You okay?" a voice called.

Travis turned around.

It was Mr. Rivera. He worked in maintenance.

"Yeah," Travis said nervously. "I think so."

"The game is over, son. Time to go home."

"Yeah," Travis said as he left the gym.

CHAPTER 8

He didn't tell Sonya or his parents what had happened in the gym. He said he didn't feel well.

"Don't you want to get something to eat?" Sonya asked as she drove him home.

"Nah," Travis said. "I'm not hungry."

He rested his head against the seat. His eyes closed. Instantly he saw the face of the emoji again. His eyes popped open.

"I'm sorry you don't feel well." Sonya put her hand on his. "I'll take you home."

"Sorry." He smiled at her. "Thanks."

Travis didn't have any intention of staying home. He needed to talk to Erik as soon as possible.

Erik scrolled through his phone. "His name is Haruto Asano," he said.

Erik wasn't shocked by Travis's story. He'd read all about the emoji. Other people had mentioned the same weird things happening.

"It can drive you crazy," Erik said. "And it doesn't stop."

They were sitting in Wager's Pizza Parlor. It was *the* pizza place. Everybody at Dyre went there. Travis and his friends always claimed a booth in the back. But tonight Erik and Travis were alone.

"Is that who created it?" Travis asked. "Why don't the police arrest him?"

"You can't arrest someone for making an emoji," Erik said, laughing.

"Why did I get it? Why is it so powerful?" Travis asked.

"I'm glad you didn't send it to me," Erik said. "But you should've sent it out."

"I wouldn't put this on anyone," Travis said.

"Yeah. Well, you put it on yourself." Erik eyed him. "The emoji is called 'unmei.' It's Japanese for *doom*. It can also mean *fate*."

"Great," Travis said.

What was he going to do? Things were going to get worse. That was his biggest fear. He couldn't handle it. It would drive him crazy.

"The creator's still alive too," Erik said.

"Haruto?" Travis asked.

Erik nodded his head.

"He lives in Los Angeles. He has a studio there. That's where he makes up this stuff. That's all I've found online."

"Do you think he will talk to us?"

"Hmm. Don't know. People say he's a recluse. He doesn't talk to anyone." Erik started reading from his phone. "*Haruto was a pioneer in HTML and XML. He won many awards for his coding skills.*"

"So he has mad skills? Why did he use them like this? So many people have suffered."

The boys looked at each other. Travis knew they had to go up to LA. He needed answers.

Erik drove with Travis on Monday. They had ditched school. The boys headed to LA. Travis wanted the craziness to stop.

The past two days had been hard. Travis couldn't sleep. He couldn't close his eyes. Every time he did, he saw the emoji. It teased him. Threatened him. Somehow he'd made it through.

Erik pulled his car into a small parking lot. Haruto's studio was in Hollywood. It was in an old brown building.

As they pulled up, the sun disappeared. The sky turned gray and ominous. It was getting chilly. Travis was glad he had worn a jacket.

"This place is a dump," Erik said.

"Yeah," Travis said. "Well, we're not here because we wanted to see something nice."

They got out of the car. A homeless man sat in a parking space. Next to him was a shopping cart. The cart was filled with stuff. It looked like blankets and old clothes. Everything was dirty.

"Spare any change?" The man smiled. He was missing a lot of teeth. His face was red. It looked scorched by the sun.

"Sorry," Travis said.

The boys kept walking.

"It's bad luck to ditch school," the homeless man said.

Travis quickly looked back at him.

"Just keep walking, dude," Erik said. "We don't need any trouble."

Haruto's studio was on the second floor. An old stone staircase was the only way up. The number on the door hung sideways. Did it mean anything?

"Should I just knock?" Travis asked.

"Yeah," Erik said. "We can't just stand here. How else would he know we're here?"

"I don't know. Maybe he just senses things."

"Just knock, Travis."

Travis knocked. There was no answer. He knocked again. Still nothing.

Then a voice asked, "Can I help you?"

Travis and Erik turned around. A man stood there. He looked young. Not a teen, but certainly still in his twenties.

"Yeah." Travis cleared his throat. "We're looking for Haruto Asano."

"He's not here," the man said.

"Do you know when he'll be back."

"Never."

"Where did he go?" Erik asked.

"That's not really your business." The man's answers were curt. It seemed like he wanted the boys to leave.

"This guy here ..." Erik pointed at Travis. "He is being stalked by an emoji."

"Erik," Travis said. "Let's—"

"That's funny," the man said. "You both need

to leave. Don't come here ever again. I've got work to do."

Then Travis realized something. This man was Haruto Asano! He was much younger than he had imagined.

"Look," Travis said. "We drove a long way."

"I'm sorry. I can't help you."

"You must know what your emoji is doing," Travis said. "It's after me. I don't want to bother you, Mr. Asano. But I need your help."

The man stared at Travis.

"Haruto was my father," the man said. "My name is Hiro. This was my father's studio. He died here. I don't know anything about his creations. I'm just cleaning this place out." He took out a key. "If you will excuse me? I don't want to be here any longer than I need to be." He pushed past them.

Travis had a pen and a scrap of paper in his pocket. He scribbled down his phone number. "Look, we don't want to bother you," he said. "My name is Travis. This is my friend Erik. Here's my number. We just want to stop this thing. It's bad. People have been hurt."

Hiro took the piece of paper. Then he went inside. The door slammed behind him.

CHAPTER 9

I hope this works," Travis said nervously. The wind had picked up. More clouds filled the sky.

He and Erik were at a cemetery. It was small. Large trees encircled it.

The boys stood by Haruto Asano's grave. The headstone was small. It read *Haruto Asano 1945–2013*. Below that was a Japanese symbol, 平和.

After leaving Hiro, they didn't know what to do. Erik's car needed gas. At the gas station they searched their phones. How could they stop bad luck? What they found didn't help.

Throw salt over your right shoulder. Duh! Too easy.

Cleanse the area where the curse's creator works. That was out. There was no way to get inside Haruto's office.

Eventually Travis found a solution. Erik thought it would work. They had to find out where Haruto was buried. It wasn't too hard. Next they needed a printer. They went to a business center.

At the business center, they paid for computer time. Travis opened his email. He found the original cursed emoji messages. Erik showed him how to see the source codes. The emojis and text became numbers and symbols. Travis printed both emails showing only the source codes.

The two then went to a convenience store. They purchased some matches. Finally the boys went to the cemetery. Haruto's grave was easy to find.

"This will work," Erik said. "You just have to believe it."

To break the curse, they had to burn the code. The ash from the burned paper had to be left on the grave.

"Please. Please. Let this be over. Put this curse back with its creator," Travis said.

He set the paper on fire. The flame was slow to catch. Then it burned hot and fast.

"It's supposed to," Erik said. "You're coming full circle."

"Ashes to ashes? Dust to dust? Is that what I'm supposed to say," Travis asked. He dropped the flaming papers.

"Sounds good to me," Erik said.

The papers burned down to ashes. A little pile of gray dust was left behind.

The boys looked at each other.

"How do you feel?" Erik asked. "Like you ended an old curse?"

"No," Travis said. He seemed upset. "That's

the problem. This curse isn't old. We're trying to get rid of an emoji. It's of this century. And it is really sticking it to people."

The boys stood at the grave for a few minutes.

A ray of sunlight poked through the gloom. It shined right on them. Sunlight filled the cemetery.

"Well," Erik said. "That's a good sign anyway."

CHAPTER 10

Travis slept soundly that night. He didn't dream about the emoji. It was his first good night's sleep in days.

Buzz. Buzz.

It was Travis's phone. The buzzing woke him up. Was it Sonya? They had texted the day before. But they hadn't spoken for more than a day. Yesterday had wiped him out. He didn't talk to anyone after he got home.

Travis grabbed his phone. It was a text from Erik.

ERIK: In the hospital! Hit by a car last night. Bummed!

What? Travis had to read it again. He couldn't believe it. His heart started pounding. He couldn't catch his breath.

Haruto's emoji curse hadn't been lifted at all!

"I was walking with my mom," Erik said. "I heard a screech. Then it hit me. I don't remember anything after that."

Erik was lying in a hospital bed. His arm had a cast. He had a leg cast too. His broken leg was elevated by a pulley and splint. Erik had a few bruises. He looked beat up.

He had gone shopping with his mom. A car struck him in the parking lot.

"Good thing your mom's okay," Travis said.

"Yeah."

"What about the person who hit you?" Travis asked. "What will happen to them?"

"It was an accident. The driver said he just lost control."

"How do you lose control in a parking lot?"

Erik shrugged. The boys stared at each other. Machines made beeping sounds in the room.

"Travis," Erik said. "Is it the curse? What are we going to do?"

"I don't know," Travis said.

Travis wanted to blow off school. But he couldn't. He was cursed. There was no way out. Who could he ask for help? He wanted to talk to Sonya or his parents. But he didn't want them to get hurt.

Tony got hurt playing football. But Tony was living his own curse. At least that's what Travis supposed. Tony had also rejected the emoji.

Then Travis's dad totaled his car.

Bronson took over as the basketball team's star player.

Travis had blown it with UCLA's scout.

And then there were the horribly real dreams.

Now Erik was in the hospital.

Travis knew the bad dreams would come back. He was frightened. Would he have to leave town? What would happen next?

Sonya had sent many texts. Travis ignored them. She finally caught up to him before lunch.

"Crazy about Erik, huh?" she said.

"Yeah," Travis said. He tried not to make eye contact. Sonya knew Travis too well. She had to know something was off.

"Let's eat," she said.

"I can't," he said. "I missed yesterday. I have to catch up in the library."

"I can help you," she said, smiling. Sonya had a great smile. It was warm. Caring. He hoped he could still make their anniversary special.

Travis wanted to tell her everything. But he couldn't. She would get hurt.

"No," he said as he walked away. "Please go eat. I'll call you after practice."

"Okay." She stared at him, confused.

It was basketball practice. Travis couldn't focus. Not that it mattered. Bronson dominated the court. Nobody noticed Travis.

He couldn't stop thinking about the curse. His life was ruined.

The team ran through a drill.

He had the ball. Bronson guarded him. His smile was sly.

Travis was pissed. He was better than this. Basketball was his life. He was smart. The curse had made him weak. Made him doubt himself.

He faked right. Then he spun left. The other players were too slow.

The ball thudded off the backboard. Then it went through the net. He had made a layup.

Yes! He still had it. Now everyone else knew it too. His teammates slapped his back. Bronson frowned.

It was on.

CHAPTER 11

Travis walked home. The sun had started to set. He felt giddy. His pace quickened. The curse had not beaten him down today.

"Maybe the curse is in my mind," he said out loud.

Positive thinking helped. But how else could he shake this curse? His head played a part. And he hadn't had a nightmare yet. Was that it?

As he walked, he heard a noise. He looked

at the houses around him. Nobody was outside. There weren't any cars on the street.

The noise got louder. Then even louder. He looked behind him. There was a black luxury SUV with tinted windows. It was following him!

Travis started to run. The SUV's engine roared. It chased after him. He ran across the street. The SUV was behind him.

He ran up to a house. "Help! Help!" he called as he pounded on the door.

There was no answer.

The SUV was parked at the curb. Travis took off again. The SUV pulled out in front of him.

"Leave me alone!" he yelled.

The SUV stopped. Its driver's-side door opened.

Travis was stunned.

It was Hiro.

CHAPTER 12

The coffee shop was crowded. People were getting off work. High school and college students hogged the tables.

"You have to understand," Hiro said. He took a sip of coffee. "My father was not an evil man."

Travis nodded. He drank some water.

Travis wanted to go somewhere more private. But Hiro liked crowds. He said it was because of the emojis.

"They don't want to be seen," he said. "They

prey on loneliness. I went online. Looked at some chat rooms. I made suggestions. Try not to be alone. Ever. That's the most important. I don't know if it helped anyone."

"Why did you come to me?" Travis asked.

"My father was a big hit," Hiro said. "He created many websites. In his hands the Internet seemed alive."

Hiro glanced away. Travis could tell he missed his father. He sensed that Haruto had not been an evil man.

"My father was idealistic. He didn't work for cash. My father worked because he loved his family. He had a great job, but he wasn't happy. So he quit. Started his own business. He rented that office in Hollywood. Then my older brother died. His name was Kenzo."

Hiro eyed Travis.

Travis had been lucky. Nobody close to him had died. He supposed he took it for granted. He was blessed to have his family.

"Kenzo was my father's favorite." Hiro stared out the window. "It never bothered me. My brother was good at everything. He got good grades. He was a great athlete. Everybody loved him. Then he got sick. He caught a cold. Can you believe it? It escalated. In two weeks he was dead."

Travis sipped his water. The talk made him nervous. He didn't know how to feel about the information.

Curses?

Hiro's family?

He was just a high school junior. His biggest problem was getting into a good college. But that was before the emoji ...

"My father couldn't accept it," Hiro went on. "He didn't accept Kenzo's death. How could such a strong person go from healthy to dead? Something else was at work. Something bigger. What was God's plan? My brilliant father decided to get to the bottom of it. So he tried to talk with my dead brother. He got into mysticism. Witchcraft. Séances ..."

Hiro looked at Travis. The man seemed relieved. How long had he waited to tell the truth? Since his father's death?

"That's when my father attracted evil spirits. And we are dealing with those spirits now, Travis."

CHAPTER 13

Travis's mom called during the meeting. Where was he? Why wasn't he home? He was usually home much sooner. Travis got off the phone. That was when Hiro insisted on driving him home.

"So why contact me?" Travis asked as they drove.

"I know what it's like to worry," he said.

Travis thought the SUV was plush. Everything about it was state of the art.

"As I said," Hiro stated. "My father was not

a bad man. I believe those evil spirits tricked him. Maybe they convinced him to make the emoji. Perhaps they promised him revenge. He was angry with the doctors who couldn't save my brother. But my father wouldn't have to do the dirty work."

Hiro looked at Travis. Travis still didn't know what to think.

"I think the spirits convinced my father to create the emoji. And then to email it."

"But why use emojis at all?" Travis asked. "Why couldn't the spirits just do it themselves?"

"They needed a vessel," Hiro said. "That was my father. Through him, they used email. It is just like a chain letter. You wouldn't remember those. But people used them to spread bad luck. Emojis are cute and fun. How could they be bad? You didn't take them seriously, right?"

"No. I thought it they were silly."

"Exactly. Evil spirits depend on it. They want us to think they are harmless. That's how they prey on people."

The two drove in silence.

"Do you think they killed your father?" Travis asked.

"Yes," Hiro said. "I can't prove it, of course. My father was a healthy man. I think he wanted revenge. But then he changed his mind. The good in him thought twice. He told me he was done with them. Then he mysteriously died of a heart attack."

Travis didn't know what to say.

"I am asking for your help."

"How can I help?" Travis asked.

"You can help me delete the code. It's on my father's computer."

"But … why me? Why not other people that have been cursed?"

"People like to talk on social media," Hiro said. "They make bold statements. Most of the time they never do anything. You and your friend are the only people who have tracked down my father. Some have emailed. But you two came to my father's studio."

"Can't you delete the code from your computer?" It was the simplest way.

"The code originated from my father's computer. We need to delete the code. Then we'll destroy the computer. The code will be gone. And any connection it has to my father will be gone. The evil will stop. Then the souls of my family can rest. That's all I want."

Travis realized something. What he had tried with Erik hadn't worked. That's why the cemetery ceremony had failed. They could sprinkle paper ashes on Haruto's grave forever. The spirits would never leave. They lived in a safe place. Haruto created it for them.

"Can I think about it?" Travis asked. He needed time to process.

"Of course," Hiro said. "I understand. But you want this nightmare to end. So do I."

CHAPTER 14

Travis couldn't think straight after talking with Hiro. He couldn't concentrate on homework. The bed looked inviting. He would rest his head, just for a second. Homework could wait till the morning.

In moments he was asleep.

In what felt like seconds, his eyes flew open. Sunlight streamed through the blinds.

Was it morning? Travis eyed his phone. It was almost 8:00 a.m. He would be late for school! He grabbed his backpack and quickly left his room. Travis went downstairs. His parents watched TV in the living room.

"Hey," he said.

They didn't respond. His parents never watched TV in the morning. They didn't have time.

Then he noticed what was on the screen.

It was the emoji. Its mouth moved up and down. Was it laughing? There was no sound.

Travis's parents started to laugh.

Wait! Was he dreaming?

He didn't have time to wake himself up.

Zap!

Travis stood in the middle of his school's campus. Students walked to class. Others texted. Even more gathered in small groups. Travis was frozen, his backpack slung over his shoulder.

He noticed something odd. Some students weren't students at all. They had flat emoji faces! They looked like the second emoji. There were the same red teeth. And one eye was open.

"Wake up!" Travis yelled.

He got nervous. His heart thumped. Wake up! Wake up! He didn't want to see how this nightmare ended.

Zap!

Suddenly he was in the middle of a basketball game. It was in the high school gym. There was a huge crowd of fans.

Travis wore his team uniform. The opposing team wore black and red. They took the ball and ran. The Dyre team followed.

Travis watched passively. The other team scored.

The crowd cheered.

Travis looked around. Many fans had flat emoji faces. Where was Sonya? He didn't see her. He saw Erik and Carla. Their faces were flat and lifeless too.

"No!" he screamed.

The buzzer sounded.

The players stopped moving. Fans froze.

Travis could hear a whisper. Then it grew louder.

"Travis! Travis! TRAVIS!" the voices called.

The flat faces stared at him.

Then everyone stood. In an instant they began to move. They were coming for him!

Travis tore out of the gym. He ran across the school parking lot. The crazed people burst out of the gym. They chased him and chanted his name.

Travis approached the entry to the parking lot. Suddenly Sonya's red car appeared.

The door flew open.

"Come on in, Travis!" She smiled.

Travis shrieked in horror. Sonya's face was flat! It was the emoji!

"Aahh!" he yelled, trying to run.

Zap!

It was pitch black. His clock read 11:34 p.m. Where was he? What had just happened?

Travis looked around his room.

He was panting. His body was drenched in sweat.

Once he calmed down, he sent a text.

TRAVIS: [I will help you!]

Travis ditched school again. He borrowed Erik's car. LA was his destination.

Sonya had sent a few texts.

SONYA: [Where are you?]

[HELLO? Are you still my boyfriend? ;)]

Travis felt bad. He wished he could talk to her about this. Nobody else could get hurt. Especially people he cared about.

Hiro's plan had better work.

"Excuse the mess," Hiro said. He stood at the door of his father's studio. "My father had a lot of interests."

The studio was packed. There were magazines and books. Tech included tablets and laptops. Newspaper clippings were tacked on the wall.

Some were about virtual reality. Others were comic strips. There were even stock market graphs. The floor was littered with paper.

A desktop computer sat on a wooden desk. Sticky notes were everywhere. A layer of dust covered everything.

"This place is filthy," Hiro said.

"It's not too bad," Travis said.

"I've started cleaning. But we need to stop the emoji first."

The two stared at the computer. It seemed harmless. Would it even boot up?

"So," Travis said slowly. "What now?"

"We turn it on," Hiro said. "Thank you again for helping my family."

Hiro pressed the power button. The desktop unit hummed. He typed on the keyboard.

Suddenly the room spun to the left! The ceiling stayed put. But the entire room had shifted. Loose papers flew around. Somehow the computer didn't move.

Travis was knocked to the floor.

"I just need to find the file!" Hiro gasped.

Travis couldn't believe it. What had just happened? Did anyone else feel it? Was it an earthquake? No. That wasn't it.

Hiro continued typing.

The room flipped upside down! Then it flipped back. This time things stayed in place. Weird!

"Got it!" Hiro yelled. "Emoji codes are simple," he said. His finger hovered over the delete key. He started hitting it over and over.

The code's black letters started to disappear.

Travis's heart pounded.

Hiro's face slammed against the computer screen! "Aahh!" he shouted. His nose was bloodied.

"Hiro!" Travis yelled. He tried to approach. But he was pulled away.

Thud!

Travis slammed into the wall. The force knocked the wind out of him. He tried to stay calm.

The emoji appeared in the studio's window. It was missing one of its white eyes.

"You deleted part of it!" Travis yelled.

Hiro continued to erase the code.

The emoji was no longer smiling. Its teeth appeared a lighter red.

Then the studio started to spin. The spinning was slow. But then the pace picked up. Travis couldn't move. He was pressed against a wall.

Hiro remained in front of the computer. But Travis saw that his fingers weren't on the keyboard.

The emoji's black face grew. It was no longer flat. Was it inflating like a beach ball? Its mouth opened and closed.

The studio's windows shattered.

The emoji moved toward Hiro. Its large jaws unhinged.

"No!" Travis screamed.

There was nothing he could do. Travis was certain he would be next.

The front door flew open. Sunlight poured in. A silhouette appeared in the doorway.

"Travis!"

It was Sonya.

CHAPTER 15

Sonya? Run!" Travis yelled.

Sonya stared at him. Why wasn't she spinning too? Maybe only Haruto's studio was spinning. Nobody else knew what was happening.

The emoji eyed Sonya. It smiled. Then it turned and moved toward her.

Oh no! It was three-dimensional. It had always looked flat before. Like how people would see it on a computer screen.

Sonya stared at the emoji. Her jaw dropped. She was in a trance. The emoji opened its mouth.

It was going for her now!

"No!" Travis screamed.

Travis flew at the thing. He grabbed the emoji. It felt solid. But then he started to sink into its mass!

Hiro pounded the computer keyboard.

Travis saw the last portion of code disappear. He steadied himself. He no longer felt like he was sinking.

A ray of white light shot out from the computer screen. It zapped Hiro in the chest. His body flew across the room. He landed with a thud.

The emoji got smaller. It was screaming as it shrunk.

Travis looked at the computer. More emoji code appeared on the screen. The computer regenerated it. No! The evil spirits were still inside.

Travis moved to the desk. He picked up the computer and threw it against the wall. It exploded.

He grabbed Sonya just before they were knocked to the ground.

"Are you okay?" he asked.

"Travis!" Sonya pointed.

The computer was in flames. Two spirits appeared. They were Haruto and Kenzo. The two stood over the fallen Hiro.

"All he wanted was for your souls to rest," Travis said.

The spirits looked at Travis. Then they looked back at Hiro.

Then their ghostly spirits dived into Hiro's body. They reemerged a few seconds later and soared upward. Then they disappeared.

Hiro sat up. He looked at Travis and Sonya.

"I think we did it," Hiro said. "I think we stopped the bad spirits."

"I hope so," Travis said. He looked at Sonya. "I'm sorry I didn't tell you about this," he said. "I couldn't risk it. I didn't want you to get hurt."

Sonya stared at him in disbelief.

"Are you mad?"

She shook her head. Then she gave him a big hug. He held on to her. He could feel her heart pounding. His heart pounded twice as hard.

Buzz. Buzz. Buzz.

It was his phone. Where was it? It continued to buzz. There it was! Under the burned out computer.

Travis wasn't taking any chances. That computer had been possessed. He kicked the broken pieces away. Then he poked his phone with his foot.

It was Erik. Travis picked up the phone. "Hey," he said. "We did it!"

"You did?" Erik sounded relieved. "Awesome! Look, bro, don't be mad. I told Sonya where you were. She was buggin', dude. I had to tell her what was up. I think she may be coming to stop you."

Travis looked over at Sonya and smiled.

"She's here," he said.

"Are you guys okay?"

He looked around the destroyed studio. It was a disaster. Then he eyed Hiro and Sonya.

"Yeah. I think we finally are."

Travis sat at his computer. He read over an email. The clock read 5:13 p.m. Two more hours before he had to be at Sonya's. He still needed to shower. Then he would put on his suit and head over.

His life had come full circle. Erik was making a speedy recovery. He barely needed crutches. Travis's father had gotten a work promotion. He had just purchased an even cooler car than the one that got totaled.

People who had been cursed also seemed to be doing better. Erik had looked at some online posts. Things were looking up.

Travis was more focused. Even his basketball had improved. Bronson had slowly become just another person on the team. Travis realized his rival made the team better. They were working together now.

There were no signs of the emoji of doom. No bad dreams. Travis barely gave the evil spirit another thought. Why waste his time?

Hiro had called to check in. He'd told him that Haruto's studio was now empty. Hiro saw no evidence that the evil emoji would return. "I couldn't have done it without your help," he'd said.

Travis wanted to email more college scouts. He would contact as many as he could. Choosing only two colleges had created too much pressure. Now he had many more on his dream list. He felt good about his decision.

He clicked send. There! He hoped this email would lead to something big. Maybe a scout would come take a look.

He checked his phone. No voice mails. Time to get ready. He went to shower. As he got up, his phone buzzed. An incoming message!

An emoji appeared! He hadn't even opened the message. What?!

This emoji was black with red eyes.

The phone buzzed. The vibrations became stronger. The phone hopped and jumped on the table.

The emoji's eyes glowed. Travis could make out the faces of Haruto and Kenzo. They were not smiling. They were screaming.

The emoji grew. The phone's screen began to crack.

Then the new emoji erupted from the phone ...

WANT TO KEEP READING?

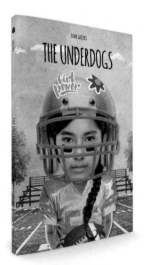

9781680211443

Turn the page for a sneak
peek at another book in the
White Lightning series:

THE UNDERDOGS

CHAPTER 1

LUNCH GAME

Jasmine Le's eyes narrowed. She was watching Mark Kline play football. It was lunchtime. Mark and some other guys were playing.

A blond thirteen-year-old god. Wow! she thought.

"Oh man!" Mark yelled. "You blew it."

He was looking at Mike Ramirez. Mike had missed a pass. The ball was on the ground. It had landed close to Jasmine.

Her BFFs were sitting on some bleachers behind her. Zoe Ebad and Tess Quade. Zoe was a tall and perfect blonde. "Do you ever get pimples? I've never seen one on your face. Unfair!" Tess once told her.

Tess's hair was long and brown. She had smooth dark skin.

Jasmine was a hybrid of the two. Long black hair. Olive skin.

Everyone on the field was in eighth grade. They went to Meadow Springs Middle School.

"Shouldn't you throw the ball back?" Zoe asked.

Jasmine wasn't a tomboy. But there were only boys on her street. She had played kickball with them. Baseball, soccer, and even tackle football too. She grabbed the football. Then she threw it back.

"Oh my gosh!" Zoe said, laughing. "You did it. I can't believe it."

"Did you think she wouldn't?" Tess asked.

The ball soared through the air. The boys watched it. Mark barely moved to catch it.

"Nice throw," Mark said. "For a girl."

"Nice throw, period," Jasmine said.

Mark laughed. "All right. Let's get in our formations," he called. "We still have fifteen minutes till the bell rings."

"Are you going to eat your lunch?" Zoe asked. She held up Jasmine's sandwich. "It looks good."

"Eat it," Jasmine said. "I'm going to play football."

Tess and Zoe looked at each other. "I don't recall them asking you to play," Tess said.

"So?" Jasmine smirked. She walked out onto the field. Jasmine planted herself between the two teams. The boys started yelling. She tuned it out. Mark stared at her. She didn't even blink.

"What are you doing?" Mark asked.

"I want to play football," Jasmine said. "I'm just as good as any of you."

"But you're a girl." Mark frowned. "You can't play football!"

"Why not? I play with boys a lot. I've even played tackle football."

"You're a girl!" Mark said again. "You will get hurt."

"No, I won't!"

The other boys yelled too. They told Jasmine to get off the field. Tess and Zoe ran over.

"Jasmine," Zoe said. "Come on!"

"Ignore our friend," Tess said to Mark. "She ate lunch in the cafeteria. Bad food makes you weird."

"I'm feeling fine," Jasmine said. "If boys can play football, we can too."

"Mr. Ross," the boys called.

Mr. Ross was in charge of school security. The man was short and stocky. He always wore tracksuits. Maybe he had played high school football. But he was out of shape now.

"What's the problem here?" Mr. Ross asked.

"Jasmine thinks she can get in on this game. Play football with us," Mark said.

"I *can* play football," Jasmine said. "They just won't let me."

Mr. Ross stared at them. "Um. Now listen, Jasmine." Mr. Ross stopped talking. He looked like he was thinking. "These boys are playing football. It's not the game for you."

"Why not?"

"Well. Um … because you're a girl."

"That's not a reason. Sex doesn't matter. I can play," Jasmine insisted.

"Get her off the field, Mr. Ross!" one player yelled.

"Look," Mr. Ross said. "You must get off—"

"No!"

Silence.

Mr. Ross was known for being nice. But he did have a temper. "Leave this field, or go see the principal. It's up to you."

Jasmine held her ground. But Zoe stepped

in. "We were just leaving," she said. Zoe grabbed Jasmine's arm. "Enjoy your game," she yelled to the boys.

Tess grabbed Jasmine's other arm.

The girls led her off the field.

The rest of lunch passed in silence. Jasmine sat on the bleachers with Tess and Zoe. She watched the game. What would it be like if she were allowed to play?

"Stop being so mad," Zoe said. "You want to play football? Since when?"

"Since those boys wouldn't let me," Jasmine said.

Jasmine fumed the rest of the day. No way would she take no for an answer. Girls could play football. They could if they wanted to play.

The friends met up after school. They always walked home together.

"Look," Tess said. "That shirt is so cute." Tess

showed the girls her phone. The cool shirt was on Instagram.

"Do you like it, Jazz?" Tess asked Jasmine.

Jasmine eyed the shirt. It was white. "I'm Not Hot" was written on it. "It's cool," Jasmine said.

But Jasmine kept thinking about football. Zoe and Tess talked. Jasmine thought about justice. Then something caught her eye. They were near Wagner Park.

There was Mark. Again. It was football practice. Looked like a Pop Warner team. She could see the team name. The Marauders.

Their coach was tall. He was dressed like Mr. Ross.

Jasmine had a thought. "Wait! I've got an idea," she said. She walked over to the field.

"Here we go again," Zoe said, rolling her eyes.